Text © Petronella Breinburg 1973
Illustrations © Errol Lloyd 1973
ISBN 0 370 02025 1
Printed in Great Britain for
The Bodley Head Ltd
9 Bow Street, London W C 2 E 7 A L
by William Clowes Ltd, Beccles and London
First published 1973
Reprinted 1975, 1983

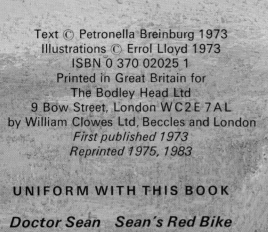

UNIFORM WITH THIS BOOK

Doctor Sean   Sean's Red Bike
Sally-Ann's Umbrella   Sally-Ann in the Snow
Sally-Ann's Skateboard

My Brother Sean

By PETRONELLA BREINBURG

With illustrations by ERROL LLOYD

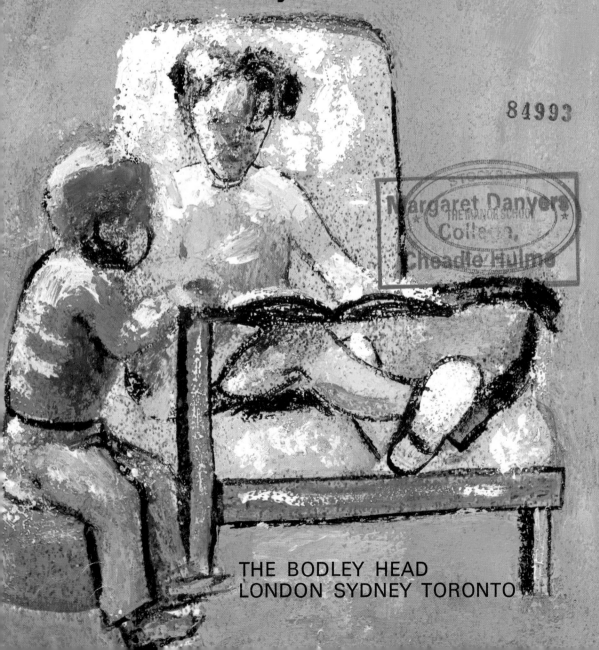

THE BODLEY HEAD
LONDON SYDNEY TORONTO

Sean always wanted
to go to school.

Then one day Mum and me
took him to the nursery.

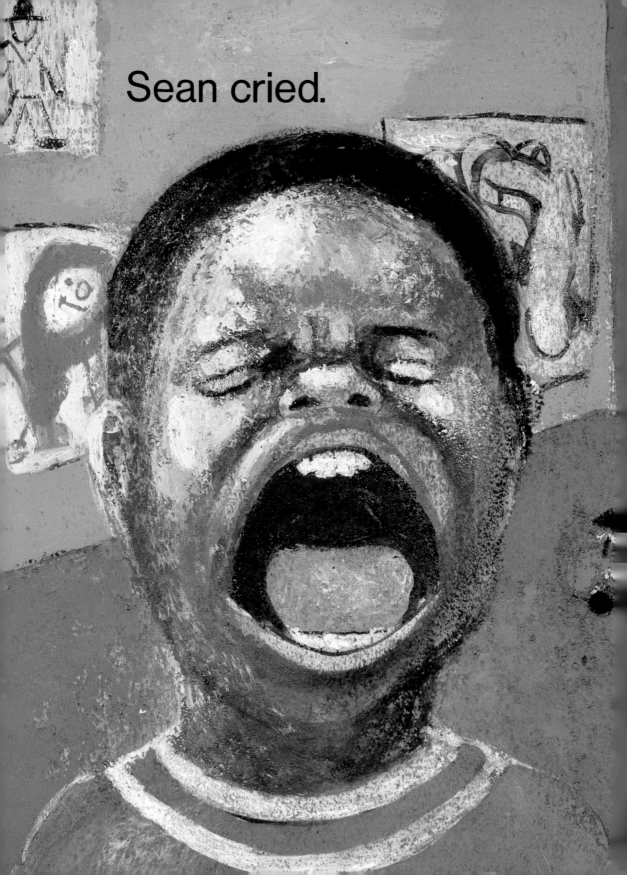

Sean cried.

At first he was only shy,

but when it was time
for us to say goodbye,

Sean cried.

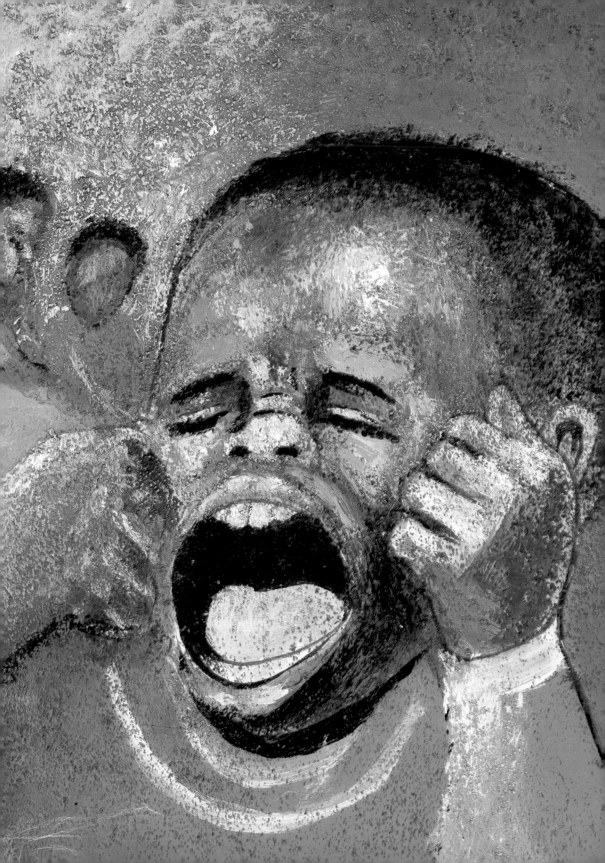

The teacher was kind.

She was fat,
just like my aunt Hillary.

"We've got lots of nice kids," said the kind teacher to Sean.

"And lots of toys,"
said Mum.

"And a donkey for riding,"

said a boy who
wanted to be friends.

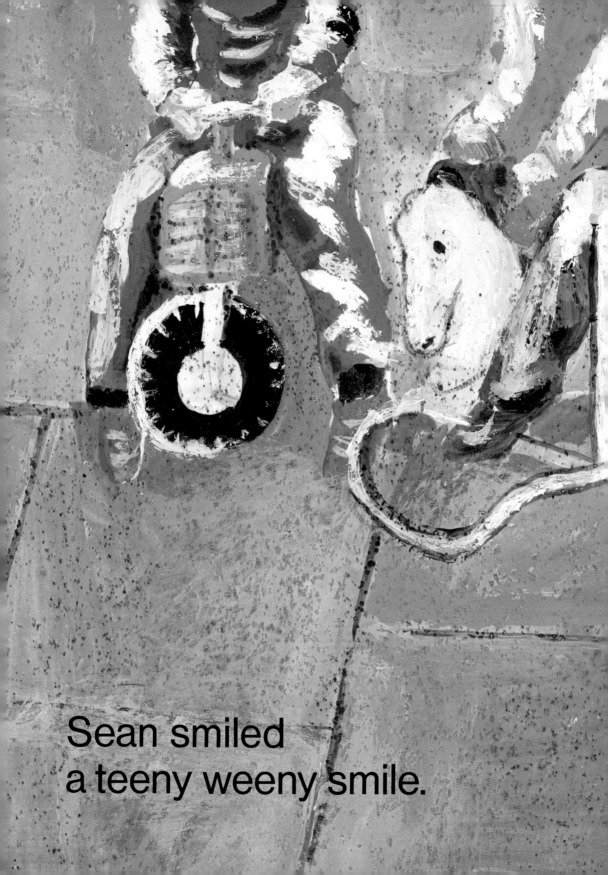

Sean smiled
a teeny weeny smile.

So Mum and me
left him at school.